Where's My Puppy?

A Story by Linda Slifka

Illustrated by Margaret Middleton

OUTLAND Books

Skaneateles, New York

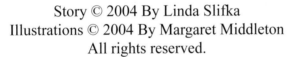

Story © 2004 By Linda Slifka
Illustrations © 2004 By Margaret Middleton
All rights reserved.

A special thanks to Donna Himelfarb for her editorial contribution.

Published by Outland Books
Outland Communications, LLC
P.O. Box 534
25 Hannum Street
Skaneateles, New York 13152

www.outlandbooks.com

ISBN: 1-932820-11-6

Printed in the United States of America

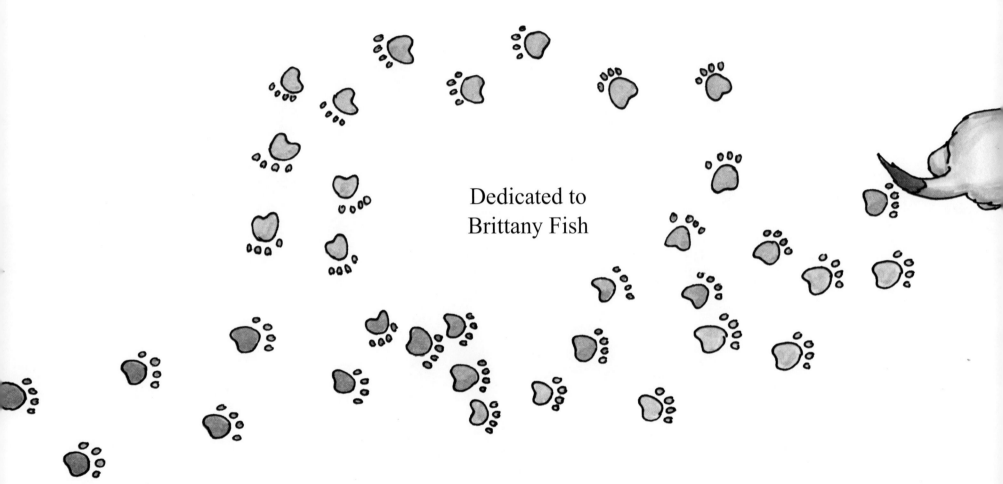

Dedicated to
Brittany Fish

For as long as he could remember, Jack had wanted a puppy of his very own.

"He would be my best friend," Jack told his parents. "We would play ball together and I would teach him tricks. He would go everywhere with me.

"Please, please, please let me have a puppy!" Jack begged.

Finally, one day, Jack's parents drove him to the animal shelter to pick out a puppy.

When Jack walked in, a very excited little puppy hurried up to the fence to greet him. Jack knew this was the puppy for him.

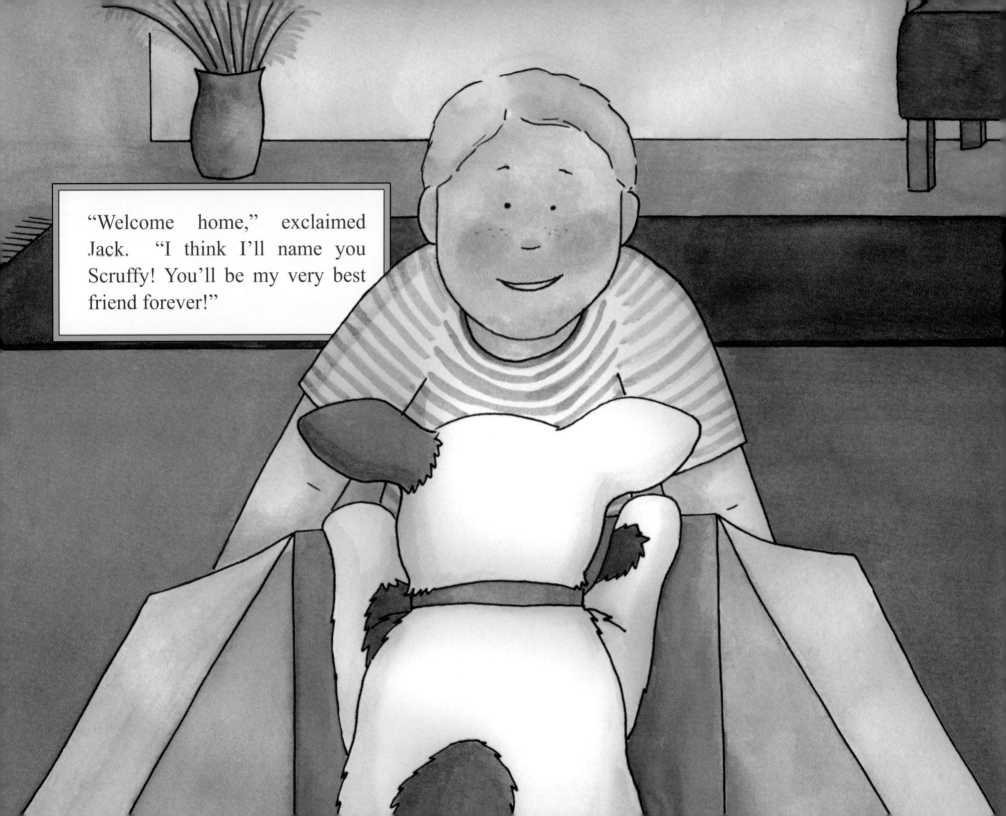

"Welcome home," exclaimed Jack. "I think I'll name you Scruffy! You'll be my very best friend forever!"

"A puppy is a lot of work," Jack's parents explained. "You have to feed him and take him for walks and give him baths but most of all, you have to keep him safe and know where he is all the time."

"I promise, I'll look after him," said Jack.

"Can Scruffy and I go play in the yard?" Jack asked his mom.

"Yes, but remember, you have to take very good care of Scruffy. A little puppy can get into *big* trouble."

"Okay mom," Jack said as he headed out the door.

Scruffy loved his new home and his new friend.

A little while later Jack's next door neighbor, Jeremy, peeked over the fence.

"Wow! A puppy! What's his name? Where did you get him? Can I play with him too?" Jeremy asked.

"His name is Scruffy and I just got him at the shelter. Let's play with him together!" Jack answered.

Suddenly the boys heard a wailing siren. They ran to the fence as a fire truck rushed by.

While the boys were watching the fire trucks, curious little Scruffy found a loose board in the fence. He wanted to see what was on the other side.

When the excitement died down, the boys realized Scruffy was missing.

"Scruffy, Scruffy, where are you?" they yelled. Jack and Jeremy looked everywhere in the yard but couldn't find Scruffy.

"Mommy, Scruffy's gone!" Jack cried.

"Oh, Jack are you sure?" his mother asked. "Weren't you watching him?"

They decided to start looking right away.

Soon everyone on the block was looking for Scruffy. Before long even the neighborhood police officer stopped to see what was going on. "Don't worry, Jack," she said, "we'll find your puppy."

"Thank you, Officer Kathy," Jack said, trying hard not to cry.

Everyone helped. They searched high and low. They even put up posters of Scruffy's picture on trees and telephone poles and in all the stores.

"Come on Jack, let's go back to the house in case Scruffy comes home," said Jack's mom. "Daddy and Officer Kathy and the others will keep searching for Scruffy."

"I know you're worried about Scruffy but he'll be back soon. Everyone is helping," she said.

Jack's dad drove his car around the neighborhood looking for Scruffy.

Officer Kathy rode for miles on her bike hoping to find the little lost puppy.

Meanwhile, Scruffy was having an adventure. At first it was exciting.

But soon Scruffy grew hungry and scared.

Then, after wandering out of town, the lost and frightened puppy found a bridge to hide under. But, before long, Officer Kathy rode by and spotted the little dog shaking by the water's edge.

"Your name wouldn't happen to be Scruffy, would it?" she asked hopefully. "A lot of people are looking for you."

Officer Kathy carefully pedaled the tired puppy home.

"Mommy, Daddy, if I got lost, would everyone be as worried about me as they were about Scruffy?" Jack wanted to know.

"Even more worried," said Jack's dad. "That's right," added his mom, "because we love you very much."

"I wouldn't want everyone to worry like that again," Jack said. "From now on, Scruffy and I are going to stay safe and sound!"

Linda Slifka is the mother of two wonderful children. She lives in a small town in the picturesque Finger Lakes area of Upstate New York and enjoys writing poetry and working in her garden.

Margaret Middleton is an artist and muralist. When not attending the Rhode Island School of Design in Providence, she lives with her family in Skaneateles, New York.

Where's My Puppy? is meant to entertain as it gently instructs young children to stay safe by not wandering from the watchful eye of their parents, even when playing close to home. The young reader is given a new perspective to better understand the loss and worry felt by the loved ones of a missing person.

Where's My Puppy? was inspired by the April 24, 2004 real-life abduction of author Linda Slifka's niece, five-year-old Brittany Fish. Miraculously, Brittany was eventually recovered and returned alive to her family in Syracuse, NY. The case has been featured twice on the Fox TV show, *America's Most Wanted*; however, as of this printing Brittany's abductor is still at large.

Renowned forensic image profiler, Jeanne Boylan, drew a composite sketch of the suspect after working with Brittany. Boylan is known for her composite images of the "Unabomber" (Ted Kaczynski), the Oklahoma City bomber (Timothy McVeigh), and Polly Klaas's abductor (Richard Allen Davis). The sketch of Brittany Fish's abductor is available at Outland Books' Web site: www.outlandbooks.com/puppy.

A portion of the proceeds from the sale of *Where's My Puppy?* will be donated to the National Center for Missing and Exploited Children.